For my brood – Abigail and Imogen – with love
G.A.

NANNY FOX
and the CHRISTMAS SURPRISE

Georgie Adams

Illustrated by
Selina Young

A Doubleday Book for Young Readers

A Doubleday Book For Young Readers

Published by
Delacorte Press
Bantam Doubleday Dell Publishing Group, Inc.
1540 Broadway
New York, New York 10036

First published in Great Britain in 1996
by Orion Children's Books
a division of the Orion Publishing Group Ltd.
Orion House
5 Upper St. Martin's Lane
London WC2H 9EA

Doubleday and the portrayal of an anchor with a dolphin are
trademarks of Bantam Doubleday Dell Publishing Group, Inc.

Text copyright © 1996 by Georgie Adams
Illustrations copyright © 1996 by Selina Young

Cataloging-in-Publication Data is available from the U.S. Library of Congress.
ISBN 0-385-32281-X

The text of this book is set in 17-point Garamond Light
Book design by Tracey Cunnell
Manufactured in Italy

October 1996
10 9 8 7 6 5 4 3 2 1

It was Christmas Eve and Arnold Fox was helping the chicks wrap presents.

Mrs. Buff Orpington was keeping a beady eye out for other foxes. It was about this time last year that the next-door hens had disappeared.

With Arnold, of course, it was different. She *had* taken a risk letting him look after her chicks, but he had proved himself to be the perfect nanny. Arnold was the *only* fox she could trust.

When all the gifts were wrapped, Arnold and the chicks
set off around the farmyard.

They visited the goats, the geese, and the cows.

There was a package for each of their friends.

Then they went to see the pigs.

"Just three presents left," said Arnold. "Now, who could they be for?"

"The three little pigs!" chirped the chicks.

The piglets opened their packages with squeals of delight.

But when Arnold said goodbye, the little pigs looked sad.

"Please stay," said one.

"We could play Three Little Pigs," said another.

"You could be the Big Bad Wolf!" said the third.

The chicks couldn't imagine Nanny Fox as a wicked wolf.
He was much too kind and gentle.

"I could wear a mask," said Arnold.

"We'll help you make one!" said the chicks.

So Arnold and the chicks played at the pigsty all
afternoon. They made a fierce-looking mask with sharp
teeth and a long pink tongue.

The piglets made pretend houses of straw, sticks, and bricks.

Every time Arnold said, *"Little pig, little pig, let me come in,"* the little pigs sang out, *"No, no, by the hair of my chinny chin chin!"*

"Then," said Arnold in his deepest, gruffest Big Bad Wolf voice, *"I'll huff and I'll puff, and I'll blow your house in!"*

Arnold rolled his eyes and looked very frightening. But because the little pigs knew it was Nanny Fox, it made them laugh—even when he pretended to gobble them up.

When it was time for bed, Arnold took the chicks back to
the henhouse.
He promised to read them the story of *The Three Little Pigs*
and pretended to be the Big Bad Wolf over and over again.

While all this was going on, Arnold's family, who lived in the woods, had been thinking about Arnold and the hens.

"If we want chicken for dinner," said Ma Fox, "we'll have to go to the farm."

"Arnold's there now," said Pa Fox. "It won't be easy."

"Not unless we *disguise* ourselves," said Lucy.

"What as?" asked Dennis. "Worms?"

"No, silly!" snapped Lucy. "Pa could dress up as Santa Claus . . . and we could go as reindeer!"

"I'll take a big sack for the hens," chuckled Pa.

"While I wait here with a cooking pot!" said Ma.

"When do we go?" asked Dennis.

"Tonight, of course," said Lucy. "It's Christmas Eve!"

So Arnold's family got busy right away. Ma Fox helped Lucy and Dennis with their costumes, while Pa Fox planned the raid.

Back at the farm, Mrs. Buff Orpington took one last look around the henhouse. Snow was falling. All seemed safe and quiet until . . .

she heard footsteps crunching in the snow . . .

and saw three shadowy shapes in the yard.

"Who's there?" Mrs. Buff Orpington said sharply.

"Santa Claus," said a voice. It was Pa Fox.

Mrs. Buff Orpington eyed him carefully. "Where are your reindeer?" she asked.

"There," said Pa Fox, waving a paw at Dennis and Lucy.

"Only two?" said Mrs. Buff Orpington suspiciously. "I thought there were supposed to be eight."

"The others couldn't come," said Lucy, trying not to giggle. "They were sick."

Mrs. Buff Orpington peered more closely. "What have you got in your sack?"

"Nothing . . . yet," said Pa Fox, flinging back his hood and making a grab at her. "But YOU can go in FIRST!"

Mrs. Buff Orpington screeched and squawked as the two reindeer bundled her into the sack.

"Stop flapping!" said Lucy.

"And pecking!" said Dennis, rubbing his nose.

Mrs. Buff Orpington's squalling could be heard all over the farmyard. The goats, the geese, the cows, and the three little pigs hurried across the yard to see what was the matter.

In the henhouse, the chicks jumped from their beds and huddled in the doorway.

Then Arnold, still wearing his wolf mask, sprang to the rescue.

Well! The sight of those sharp teeth and that long pink tongue gave Pa Fox the fright of his life. Arnold rushed at him, huffing and puffing and rolling his eyes.

"I'm going to GOBBLE YOU UP!" growled Arnold in his deepest, gruffest Big Bad Wolf voice.

Dennis and Lucy took one look, dropped the sack, and ran! Pa Fox tripped over his beard and rolled all the way back to the woods.

The chicks cheered. The little pigs sang, "Who's afraid of
the big bad wolf? The big bad wolf? The big bad wolf?"
And Arnold took a bow.

Just then there was a loud *SQUAWK*! and Mrs. Buff Orpington poked her head out of the sack.

"When you've all finished amusing yourselves . . . ," she said, "I should like some assistance!"

Arnold helped Mrs. Buff Orpington to her feet.

"Santa Claus and *two* reindeer indeed!" said Mrs. Buff Orpington. "They didn't have *me* fooled for a minute!"

"Of course not," said Arnold, with a knowing wink to the chicks. "Now, let's all go to bed . . . then the *real* Santa Claus will come!"